WHAT PET SHOULD I GET?

By Dr. Seuss

Beginner Books®
A Division of Random House 🏠 New York

Visit us on the Web!
Seussville.com
rhcbooks.com

Educators and librarians, for a variety of teaching tools, visit us at
RHTeachersLibrarians.com

This title was originally catalogued by the Library of Congress as follows:
Seuss, Dr., author, illustrator.
What pet should I get? / by Dr. Seuss. — First edition.
pages cm
Summary: A boy wants all of the pets in a pet store
but he and his sister can choose only one.
ISBN 978-0-553-52426-0 (trade) — ISBN 978-0-553-52427-7 (lib. bdg.) —
ISBN 978-0-399-55221-2 (ebook)
[1. Stories in rhyme. 2. Pets—Fiction. 3. Choice—Fiction. 4. Decision making—Fiction.]
I. Title.
PZ8.3.S477Wf 2015 [E]—dc23 2015011701

ISBN 978-0-525-70735-6 (trade) — ISBN 978-0-525-70736-3 (lib. bdg.)

MANUFACTURED IN CHINA
10 9 8
First Beginner Book Edition

We want a pet.
We want a pet.
What kind of pet
should we get?

Dad said we could have one.

Dad said he would pay.

I went to the Pet Shop.

I went there with Kay.

And so we went in . . .

I took one fast look . . .

I saw a fine dog who shook hands.

So we shook.

So I said,

"I want him!"

But then, Kay saw a cat.
She gave it a pat,
and she said, "I want THAT!"

Then Kay said, "Now what
do you think we should do?
Dad said to pick one.
We can not take home two."

Then what do you know?
We saw two other kinds.
NOW how could Kay and I
make up our minds?

A pup and a kitten.

They looked like good fun.

NOW which would we pick?

We could only pick one.

The cat?

Or the dog?

The kitten?

The pup?

Oh, boy!
It is something
to make a mind up.

Then I looked all around.
I saw something with wings.
I said, "Look at him!
We can pick one that sings."

But THEN . . .

"Look over there!"
said my sister Kay.
"We can go home
with a rabbit today!"

Then I looked at Kay.

I said, "What will we do?

I like all the pets that I see.

So do you.

We have to pick ONE pet
and pick it out soon.
You know Mother told us
to be back by noon."

And I could have done it.
I could have, I bet.
I could have said
what pet we should get.

BUT . . .

you know what Kay did . . .

Do you know what she did?

She said, "FISH!

FISH!

FISH!

FISH!

It may be a fish

is the pet that we wish!"

THEN . . .

I saw a new kind!

And they were good, too!

How could I pick one?

Now what should we do?

We could only pick one.

That is what my dad said.

But how could I make up

that mind in my head?

Pick a pet fast!

Pick one out soon!

Mother and Dad said
to be home by noon!

The time may be now
to make up my mind.
But who knows what other
good pets I might find?

I might find a new one.
A fast kind of thing
who would fly round my head
in a ring on a string!

Yes, that would be fun . . .

BUT . . .

our house is so small.
This thing on a string
would bump, bump into the wall!
My mother, I know,
would not like that at all.

SO, maybe some other
good kind of pet.
Another kind maybe
is what we should get.

We might find a new kind.
A pet who is tall.
A tall pet who fits
in a space that is small.

My mother might like
this pet best of them all.

If we had a big tent,
then we would be able
to take home a YENT!
Dad would like us
to have a good YENT.
BUT, how do I know
he would pay for a tent?

So, you see how it is
when you pick out a pet.
How can you make up
your mind what to get?

BUT . . .

What if we took
one of each kind of pet?
Then our house would be full
of the pets we would get.

NO . . .

Dad would be mad.

We can only have one.

If we do not choose,

we will end up with NONE.

"I will do it right now.
I will do it!" I said.
"I will make up the mind
that is up in my head."

The dog . . . ? Or the rabbit . . . ?
The fish . . . ? Or the cat . . . ?
I picked one out fast,
and then that was that.